3 1118 01104 5922

W9-BKE-295

The Ferguson Library
TURN OF RIVER BRANCH
Stamford, CT 06905   (CC Rt 4)
CHILDREN'S DEPARTMENT

NOV 1 6 1999   MAR 2 9 2000   JUL 3 1 2000

AUG 3 0 2000
SEP 2   2000

APR 1 7 2000   SEP 9   2000

JAN 5   2000   SEP 2 7 2

FEB 2   2000   MAY 5 - 2000   OCT 1 6 2000

FEB 1 1 2000   JUN 2   2000   NOV 1 0 2000

MAR 6   2000   JUN 2 4 2000

JUL   3 2000   DEC 1 3 2000

Carol Roth
Little Bunny's Sleepless Night

Illustrated by Valeri Gorbachev

North-South Books

New York · London

CHILDREN'S DEPARTMENT
THE FERGUSON LIBRARY
STAMFORD, CONNECTICUT

To Mark, Wendy, Glenn, and Larry
with love—and to the new love
of my life, Jacob Douglas—C.R.

To my parents—V.G.

Text copyright © 1999 by Carol Roth
Illustrations copyright © 1999 by Valeri Gorbachev
All rights reserved. No part of this book may be reproduced
or utilized in any form or by any means, electronic or mechanical,
including photocopying, recording, or any information storage and
retrieval system, without permission in writing from the publisher.

Published in the United States by North-South Books Inc., New York.
Published simultaneously in Great Britain, Canada, Australia, and
New Zealand in 1999 by North-South Books, an imprint of
Nord-Süd Verlag AG, Gossau Zürich, Switzerland.

Library of Congress Cataloging-in-Publication Data is available.
A CIP catalogue record for this book is available from The British Library.

The artwork consists of pen-and-ink and watercolor
Designed by Marc Cheshire

ISBN 0-7358-1069-9 (trade binding)
TB 10 9 8 7 6 5 4 3 2 1
ISBN 0-7358-1070-2 (library binding)
LB 10 9 8 7 6 5 4 3 2 1
Printed in Belgium

For more information about
our books, and the authors and artists
who create them, visit our web site:
http://www.northsouth.com

Little Bunny had no brothers or sisters.
He had his very own room with his very own bed.

But sometimes he got lonely—so lonely that he couldn't fall asleep.

One night he thought: What I need is the company of a good friend.

So he hopped next door to his good friend Squirrel.
"May I sleep here tonight?"

"Of course," said Squirrel as he welcomed him in.
Tucked all snug in bed next to Squirrel, Little Bunny
thought how lucky he was not to be alone.
"Good night, Squirrel," said Little Bunny.
"Good night, Little Bunny," answered his friend.

Falling asleep was easy, but staying asleep was not. Little Bunny was soon awakened by C-R-U-N-C-H, C-R-U-N-C-H, C-R-U-N-C-H!

"What's that noise?" he asked as he sat up in bed.

"It's just me cracking acorns," said Squirrel. "I always have a little snack in the middle of the night."

"Well, thanks for having me, but I can't sleep with all that noise!"

So Little Bunny left and hopped some more until he
reached his good friend Skunk.

"May I sleep here tonight?"

"YES! YES! A HUNDRED TIMES YES!" shouted
Skunk. "No one has *ever* asked to sleep over before!"

Afraid Little Bunny might change his mind, Skunk
quickly pulled him inside.

"This is fun," Skunk said as they got into their beds.

Shortly after, they fell asleep . . . but not for long.

Little Bunny was soon awakened by a terrible smell.
"What smells?" he asked as he jumped up.
"I'm afraid I do," said Skunk. "I forgot someone else was in my room. I got scared and sprayed."
"Well, thanks for having me, but I can't sleep with that smell!"

    So Little Bunny left and hopped some more until
he reached his good friend Porcupine.
    "May I sleep here tonight?"
    "Certainly," said Porcupine. "You take my bed and
I'll sleep on the floor."
    "Yippee!" shouted Little Bunny as he climbed
into Porcupine's bed and bounced around with
excitement.

"O-U-C-H!" he screamed. "What do you have in here?"

"It's just my quills," said Porcupine. "I lose some every now and then."

"Well, thanks for having me, but I can't sleep with those prickles!"

So Little Bunny left and hopped some more until
he reached his good friend Bear.

"May I sleep here tonight?"

"Why sure, make yourself at home," said Bear.

By now Little Bunny was so tired he just curled up
on the floor and went right to sleep.

But very soon after, Little Bunny was
wakened by a loud rumbling noise.
    Oh, no, it's thundering! he thought.
    But it wasn't thundering at all. His friend
Bear was snoring!
    "Well, I can't sleep with that snoring!"
said Little Bunny.

So he left and hopped some more until he reached
his good friend Owl.

"May I sleep here tonight?"

"Why yes, if you want to," said Owl. "Just follow me."

An exhausted Little Bunny went right to sleep, but soon he was wakened by a bright light shining in his eyes.

"PUT THE LIGHT OUT!" he shouted.

"I can't," said Owl. "I stay up reading every night. That's how I got to be so wise."

"Well, since you're so wise, could you please tell me how I'm ever going to get some sleep?"

"That's easy," said Owl. "Just go back home where you belong."

Little Bunny took his wise friend's advice.
Too tired to hop, he dragged himself home.
His bed never looked so good to him before.

He jumped right in.

"How wonderful!" he said to himself as he snuggled down. "No crunching noise, no terrible smell, no prickly quills, no snoring, and no bright lights. Just me, by myself, and peace and quiet. Now I can fall asleep!"

And that's just what Little Bunny did!